World of Cars

Written by

Catherine Daly

Illustrated by

Caroline Egan, Maria Elena Naggi, Scott Tilley,
and the Disney Storybook Artists

DISNEP PRESS

New York

To Nani, my right-hand man

Art Direction by Scott Tilley
Design by Tony Fejeran
Special thanks to Chris Schnabel

Copyright © 2008 Disney Enterprises, Inc./Pixar. Disney/Pixar elements © Disney/Pixar, not including
underlying vehicles owned by third parties; Mack is a registered trademark of Mack Trucks, Inc.; Dodge A100
is a trademark of Chrysler LLC; Dodge Dart is a trademark of Chrysler LLC; Hudson Hornet is a trademark of Chrysler LLC;
Chevrolet Impala is a trademark of General Motors; Fiat is a trademark of Fiat S.p.A.; Ferrari elements are trademarks
of Ferrari S.p.A.; Mercury is a registered trademark of Ford Motor Company; Model T is a registered
trademark of Ford Motor Company; Peterbilt is a trademark of PACCAR Inc.

Based on the characters from the movie *Cars*. Copyright © 2006 Disney Enterprises, Inc./Pixar

Printed in the United States of America

First Edition

10 9 8 7 6 5 4 3 2 1

ISBN 978-1-4231-0873-3

Reinforced binding

Library of Congress Cataloging-in-Publication data on file.

For more Disney Press fun, visit www.disneybooks.com

Table of Contents

Foreword

Everybody has a story, a history that makes us who we are, and the characters of *Cars* are no exception. When their body types and personalities first started to take shape in our minds and on the page, it wasn't enough for us to know them just as they would be within the borders of the story we were creating. We wanted to know everything about them: where they came from, what they'd been through, what brought them to Radiator Springs. We wanted to know them like we know our own friends. And as friends do, each of the *Cars* characters became a part of our story in very different ways.

We had our first encounter with Mater when we came across a rusty old tow truck in a vacant lot along Route 66. We knew immediately that a car with that much personality and soul had to be a part of our story. With Doc it was learning the great racing heritage of the 1952 Hudson Hornet. Here was a car with history and integrity that would make the perfect "grandpa car" for our town and the ideal counterpoint to the modern racing world we were going to explore. With Flo it was the images of the lovely ladies of the GM Motorama car shows. What would the car version of a 1957 showgirl be? What would she be doing now? Who would she fall in love with? Who else but Ramone—a 1959 Chevy Impala: one of the great, unique American cars, and one that would relish showing off the beautiful and exotic paint jobs of the famed Southern California lowriders. With Luigi and Guido, it started with a tire store. Naturally, a tire store would be the car version of a shoe store—we had to have one. But who would run such a place? Luigi, a Fiat 500, was the obvious choice, an Italian car with taste and charisma. And surely he would need an assistant named Guido, a tiny forklift who could only speak Italian. Then, of course, there was Lightning McQueen. Who else but a cocky young race car—literally built from the ground up to go as fast as possible—would be a better tour guide for our story? McQueen was the one car who could take us from the fast lane of the racing world to the slow Sunday-drive pace of Radiator Springs—a place the world had forgotten.

And sure enough, the more we discovered about their pasts and who they were before our story began, the more these Cars became like members of our family. We thought you also might like to know them a little better, so we put together this collection of the backstories of some of our favorite townsfolk from Radiator Springs. We hope you love them as much as we do.

- **John Lasseter**

Hoodwinked

Many years ago, way back before the Interstate was a glimmer in a steamroller's windshield, Mater didn't have a lick of rust on him. He was shiny and blue, without a dent in sight. Heck, he even had a hood.

Mater was one of the top four or five best lookin' trucks in town, if he did say so himself.

And he did. All the time!

When he wasn't towing broken-down cars and trucks, Mater loved hanging out with his cousins.

They had a truckload of fun together. Sometimes, Mater would have spittin' contests with Cousin Jud.

. . . or he'd go hubcap collectin' with Cousin Buford.

And sometimes, late at night, when everyone else in town was asleep, Mater and Cousin Cletus would go tractor tippin'!

"Tractors is so dumb!" Mater always liked to say.

But their favorite thing was to go fishing on a lazy Sunday afternoon. They'd fill their coolers with cans of ice-cold motor oil and head to the lake, drop their hooks in, and wait for a bite.

Truth be told, it was Mater who did all the fishing while his cousins did most of the relaxing!

You wouldn't believe the amazing things they'd find. . . .

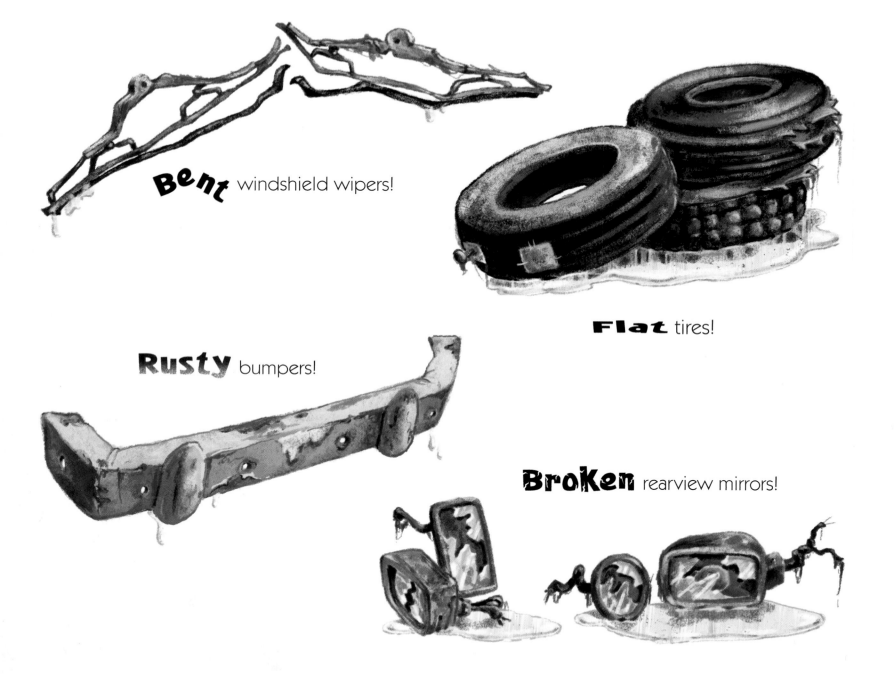

Bent windshield wipers!

Flat tires!

Rusty bumpers!

Broken rearview mirrors!

As Grammy Mater always used to say, one car's trash
was another car's treasure. And ain't that the truth!

But the stories of the ones that got away were what Mater liked best.

"That fender was *this* big," Cousin Buford always said.

Mater took his fishing very seriously. He had been practicing and practicing a new casting technique every chance he got. He couldn't wait to show it off to his cousins. One sunny afternoon, he was ready.

"I ain't braggin' or nothin'," Mater said. "But watch this!"

The cousins watched as Mater swung his tow cable twice around his cab, flipped it over his left taillight, and aimed for the water.

THUNK!

He had hooked his own hood, tore it clean off, and tossed it into the lake!

SPLASH!

His cousins stared.

"Did you mean to do that?" Cousin Buford finally asked.

"Shoot, no!" Mater cried. "I done lost my hood!"

It took a while, but they finally fished out the hood.
"Well, I'm plumb tuckered out," said Cousin Jud.
They looked at their day's catch.

FOUR
rusty windshield
wipers.

THREE
bald tires.

TWO
bent steering
wheels.

And **ONE** blue hood,
slightly dented.

It was time to call it a day.

"Well, lookee here," said a voice.

Dad-gum it, thought Mater. He didn't have to look. He knew who it was. It was Bubba, the biggest, baddest bully in town. Bubba liked to pick on cars smaller than he was. His favorite thing was to challenge them to a race. He always won, of course.

"Fishin' for junk again?" Bubba said with a sneer. Then, fast as greased lightning, he picked up Mater's hood and tossed it to his friend. "Keep-away!" Bubba shouted. Mater and his cousins raced around trying to get his hood back before it got even more dented. But Bubba and his pal were just too fast.

Finally, they grew tired of the game. But instead of giving Mater's hood back, they tossed it into a tree! "See you later, kids. It was fun playing with you!" Bubba called as they left.

"Look what he done did," Mater said dejectedly. He knew his mama was going to be madder than a wet tractor if he came home without his hood! She'd say, "Do you know how expensive hoods are, young man? Do you think they just grow on trees?"

Staring up at the tree, Mater had to laugh. It sure looked like they did!

Luckily, Red, the town fire engine, passed by just then and rescued the tree-bound hood.

Once Mater's hood was back in place, he and his cousins left the lake.

"What's that noise?" Jud asked.

"Nothin'," said Mater. But his cousin was right—his hood was making a terrible rattling racket!

"That rattlin' don't sound like nothin' to me," Jud replied.

So Mater tried squeezing his hood tight. Didn't work.

He creaked it open a little. No dice.

He zigged. Nothin' doin'.

He zagged. Same thing.

And then he had an idea so strange he thought it might work. . . .

Driving backward!
    "Whee-hee!" cried Mater.
"Kiss my grits and call me
Nancy—it works!"
    And best of all, it was more fun
than a barrel of tailpipes!
    (Mater just had to be careful not
to crash into anything.)

Soon they headed back into town.

"Uh-oh," said Cousin Cletus. "Are you seein' what I'm seein'?"

"So we meet again," said Bubba. "You got your hood back, huh?" He narrowed his eyes. "Well, I guess it's time for a race then!"

Mater gulped. Bubba leaned in so close that Mater could see the bugs in his grille. "And to make things even more interestin', the loser has to buy the winner a tank of gas. I could use some high-octane fuel!" Bubba exclaimed.

Mater gulped again. But then he smiled. He had an idea!

"I'll race you, all right," Mater said. "But are you thinkin' you can beat me if we race blindfolded?"

"Of course," scoffed Bubba.

"If we race on two wheels?"

"No problem," said Bubba.

"How 'bout if we race . . . backward?" Mater asked.

"Whatever," said Bubba. "I can beat you any day, any way."

Mater's cousins smiled.

The race course began on Main Street, wound twice around the Stanley statue, and went straight to the finish line.

Cousin Jud agreed to be the starter. "On your mark, get set, go!" he shouted. And with that, Red rang his bell.

They were off! Bubba shot into the lead, laughing away. But he soon realized that driving backward was a talent—one he didn't have! Halfway around the Stanley statue he lost control, screaming like a little scooter!

Meanwhile, Mater zipped down Main Street, spun around the statue twice, and was headed toward the finish line. That's when he saw Bubba spinning out of control!

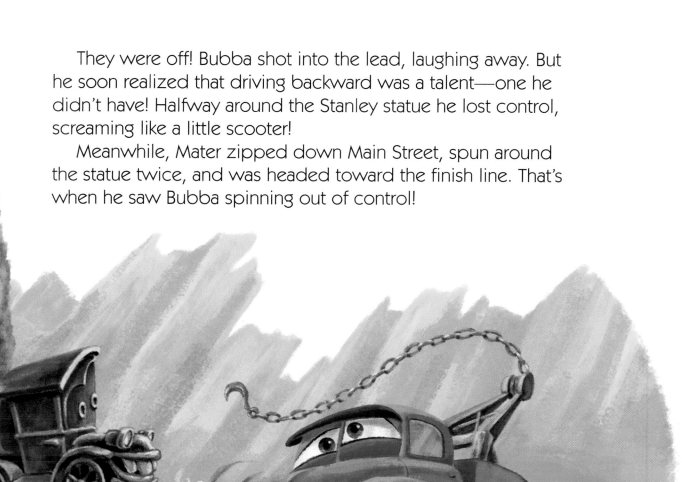

Moments later, everyone honked
and cheered as Mater won the race!

Mater was so happy he couldn't help showing off. He did a little victory dance—and his hood popped clean off.

"Dad-gum it!" Mater shouted.

"Shame on you, Mr. Tow Mater!" called a voice. "Put that hood right back on—you're in public!"

"Sorry, Mama!" Mater said.

Banged Up

Everyone knew the Fabulous Hudson Hornet. He had already won three Piston Cups—the most coveted racing trophy in the country. He held the record for the most wins in a single season. He was known as "The Champion for All Time." And he was just about to win his fourth Piston Cup. . . .

"The Fabulous Hudson Hornet heads into his final lap. The kid's gonna do it again!" the announcer said excitedly. Just then, there was a huge crash. "Oh, no! There's a four-car pileup on the track! The Fabulous Hudson Hornet swerves to avoid it . . . but Speedy Summers slams into him! The Fabulous Hudson Hornet is out of control! The Fabulous Hudson Hornet has hit the wall, hard! Folks, the race is over for the Fabulous Hudson Hornet. And maybe even his career."

When Hudson came to, he was surrounded by ambulances and reporters. There were flashbulbs going off in his face. He squinted.

"Kid, talk to me," said his crew chief.

The Fabulous Hudson Hornet opened his eyes. "Did I win?" he joked.

Everyone laughed uneasily.

"Why the long faces?" said Hudson. "I'll be good as new in no time."

The crash was in all the newspapers.

By the next season, Hudson was totally repaired. He was ready to race again.

But when he returned to the racetrack expecting a big welcome, he got the cold fender. "Sorry, kid," said his sponsor, "but you're history." They had already hired a newer model—a hotshot rookie race car.

Even though Hudson knew deep in his carburetor that he had a lot more racing left in him, he never got a chance to show anyone. There was nothing he could do. His racing days were over.

Hudson felt bad. Real bad. Racing had been his life.
"What am I supposed to do now?" he wondered out loud.
Not sure where to go, he decided to head back to the place he came from. He
figured in a city that big, he could blend in and put his racing days behind him.

But Hudson soon found out he was wrong. Dead wrong. At a stoplight, a hot rod pulled up next to him and revved his engine. "Well, if it isn't the Fabulous Hudson Hornet! Wanna race, Hud?" he asked.

Hudson glanced at the car. "Not today," he said. Then he took a closer look. "But you might want to get that left front tire aired up. It's looking pretty low."

And the next day, when Hudson stopped for some gas, a station wagon approached him, looking quite concerned. "I was so sorry to hear about your big crash, dear," she said. "You must feel just terrible. Is there anything I can do to help?"

"I'm fine, ma'am," Hudson said. Then he cleared his throat. This was going to be a bit embarrassing for both of them, but it needed to be said. "And please forgive me for being so forward," he began, "but your er, rear bumper has a loose bracket. You might want to

He couldn't even get a moment's peace at the car wash.

"Excuse me, sir, but could I take your picture?" a truck asked.

Hudson cleared his throat. "Now's not such a good time," he said. Then he squinted. "Have you had someone look at your front axle? It looks like it's bent."

BEFORE

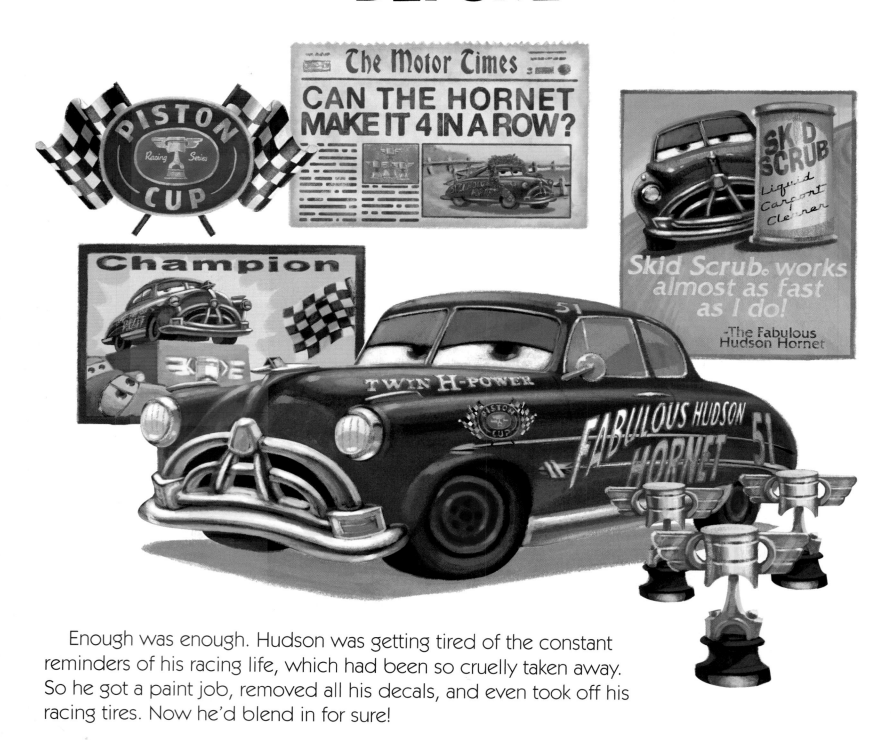

Enough was enough. Hudson was getting tired of the constant reminders of his racing life, which had been so cruelly taken away. So he got a paint job, removed all his decals, and even took off his racing tires. Now he'd blend in for sure!

MotorCity
DRIVE-IN THEATER
DOUBLE FEATURE
THREE CARS IN A FOUNTAIN
A STREETCAR NAMED DESIRE

But that didn't work either.
"Can I get your *auto*graph?" an old car
asked at the drive-in.

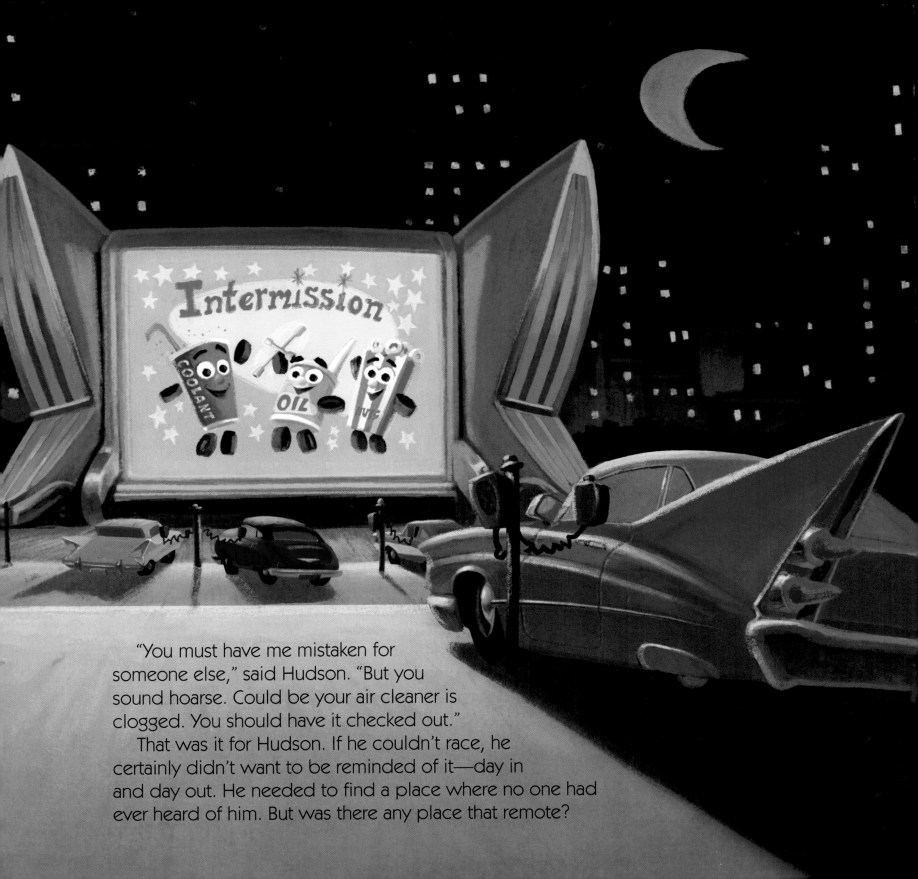

"You must have me mistaken for someone else," said Hudson. "But you sound hoarse. Could be your air cleaner is clogged. You should have it checked out."

That was it for Hudson. If he couldn't race, he certainly didn't want to be reminded of it—day in and day out. He needed to find a place where no one had ever heard of him. But was there any place that remote?

Hudson decided to take a ride on Route 66. There was so much to see—mountains, plains, cacti, monuments.

Even better, every time he stopped to look at the view, fill up on gas, or check into a motel for the night, nobody recognized him. It was great!

"I feel . . . relaxed," he said aloud to himself. He started to think that there had to be something he was good at, something besides racing.

A couple of miles outside a small town he'd never heard of, Hudson spotted a broken-down car at the side of the road. He was so deep in thought he nearly drove past him.

WHOA THERE, PARTNER!
You've just passed...
...RADIATOR SPRINGS
Jewel of the "Mother Road"!

"Well, hello, good fellow," said the car, gasping. "My name is Philip. I seem to be in a spot of trouble." He tried to start but couldn't turn over.

Hudson listened carefully. "Sounds like you're not getting any spark," he said. "I think it might be your coil wire." Luckily, he knew a quick fix. "If I may . . ."

Within moments, Philip's engine was purring again. "Cheerio!" he called as he happily pulled away. "And many thanks for your assistance!"

Hudson smiled. He felt better than he had in weeks. But he still didn't know what to do, or where to go next. He sighed and kept driving.

"That's odd," he said to himself as he read the words on a billboard in front of him.

Hudson nodded.

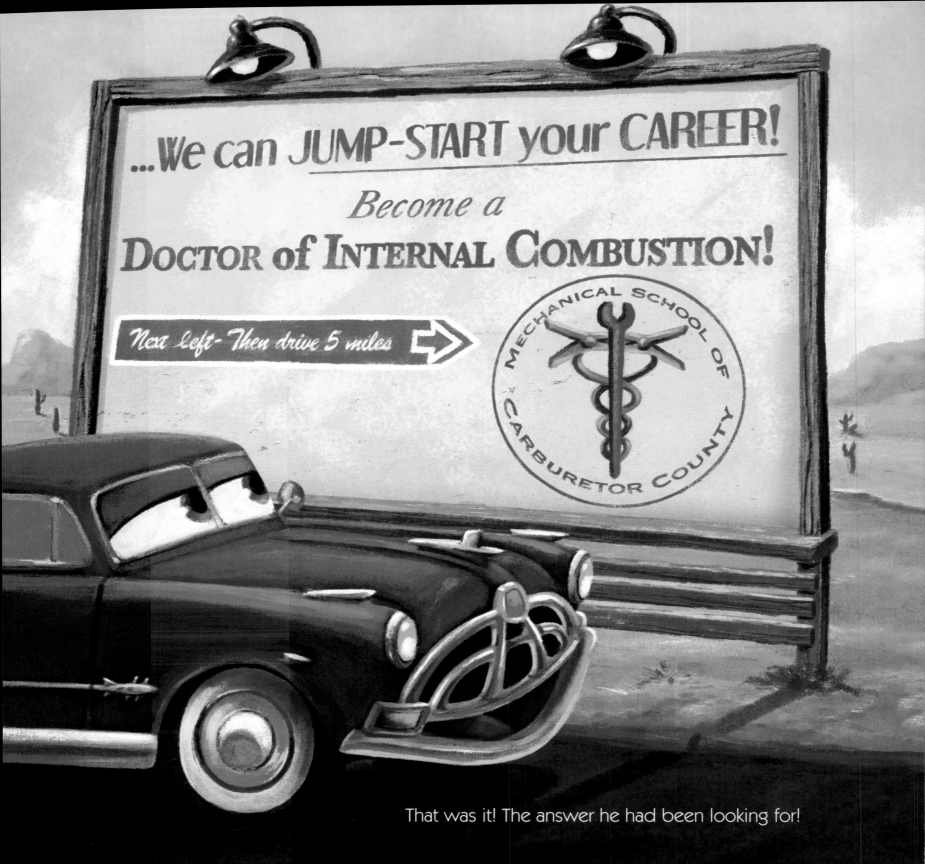

That was it! The answer he had been looking for!

Hudson took the next left and got in line to register. He felt great. He had direction—he had a purpose. And best of all, he had his privacy!

Just then, a red car tapped Hudson on the fender. "Excuse me, but do I know you?" the car asked.

Hudson sighed. "I don't think so, miss," he said, not unkindly.

"No, I'm sure of it. Wait a minute; it will come to me. . . ."

Here we go again, Hudson thought.

Finally, the car said, "I've got it! You live next door to my great aunt, Mary Jean, in Bent Fender, Arkansas!"

Hudson smiled a big smile. The old part of his life was in the past, and a new chapter was just beginning.

And that's just what happened. Hudson studied hard and graduated at the top of his class. Then he moved to a little town called Radiator Springs, the prettiest little town in Carburetor County, and set up shop there.

Folks would come from far and wide to be treated by Doc Hudson. He was the hardest working Doctor of Internal Combustion around.

The Fabulous Hudson Hornet's racing days may have been over, but Doc felt like a champion just the same.

Showstopper

Flo looked out over the Motorama floor from her spot high up on the stage. It was an amazing sight to see. The crowds! The music! The glitz! The glamour!

The Motorama was a special car show that toured from state to state displaying the newest and most advanced concept cars. It was the hottest ticket in town—if you were lucky enough to have the Motorama come to your town, that is.

Flo was the star of the show.

She even had a fan club!

Flo
fan club

No doubt about it, from her gleaming grille to her terrific tail fins, Flo was a knockout. Everyone wanted to get a look at her, and everyone wanted her photograph. There was just one problem . . .

. . . Flo was bored out of her tires. Sure, life in the Motorama was glamorous, and most cars would have given their rearview mirrors to be in the show.

But nobody realized that there was a big price to pay for being in the Motorama. Flo felt like she was living life on the shoulder—never allowed to do anything that might result in a nick or a scratch, always traveling in the back of a transport truck, and never seeing anything in any of the states she visited except for the inside of the *car*vention center. She didn't even have a garage to call her own.

Worst of all was the Motorama chaperone, Ms. Victoria. She was very strict and had lots of rules. And that meant Flo and the rest of the girls weren't allowed to have any fun at all.

Ms. Victoria's
Rules for Comportment

1. No Idling

2. No Revving

3. Unleaded fuel ONLY! NO fattening high-test, please!

4. Eight hours beauty rest per night minimum

5. And absolutely, positively, NO CRUISING!!!

One day, on the way to the next Motorama show, Ms. Victoria felt ill. (She was backfiring in a quite unladylike way, if truth be told.)

"Mitch!" she called. She asked Mitch, the truck that transported Flo and the rest of the girls—Laverne, Rhonda, and Sheila—to pull over immediately.

"Yes, ma'am," Mitch answered. He was as afraid of Ms. Victoria as the girls were. He stopped in a small town none of them had ever heard of. They all piled out of the back of the truck.

"Radiator Springs. Is this place even on the map?" asked Ms. Victoria. She backfired again. "Oh, excuse me."

The girls followed Ms. Victoria to Doc Hudson's office. They waited outside while she had a thorough examination.

Then Doc came out and said, "You'll be staying here overnight, girls. Ms. Victoria needs a new fuel pump."

The girls peeked inside to wish Ms. Victoria well. She was high up on the lift.
"Will you be okay without me?" she asked worriedly.
"Yes, ma'am," they said.
Ms. Victoria called after the girls. "Don't talk to strangers! Look both ways at every intersection! And absolutely, positively, no cruising allowed!"

"I can't believe Ms. Victoria won't be with us tonight. What will we do without her?" asked Laverne.

Flo looked at the girls and smiled. "Have fun?" she answered.

They all laughed.

The first thing they did was fill up—on high-test gasoline! Calories be darned!

Next, they stopped at Ramone's House of Body Art. "I've always wanted to get a pinstripe," Sheila said shyly.

"You've come to the right place," said Ramone. Then he painted a delicate stripe on Sheila.

"Now what?" asked Rhonda.

"Oh, I know," said Ramone. "I'll take you ladies cruising! Low and slow, that's the way to go!"

The girls gasped. They'd already broken so many rules.

"Come on, girls," said Flo. "You only live once!"

They cruised up and down Main Street all night long. Low and slow, of course!

Hours later, Ramone had an idea. "There's nothing like a sunrise over Willy's Butte," he suggested.

The girls followed Ramone to Ornament Valley to watch the sun come up. It was the most exciting day any of them had had in a long time. Especially Flo.

"It was nice to meet you, Ramone," said Flo sadly. "I had a great time."

"Low and slow, baby. Don't you forget it," replied Ramone. He was very sorry to see her go.

Later that morning, the girls nervously checked each other over before heading to Doc's to pick up Ms. Victoria.

"Uh-oh," said Laverne.

Flo had a scratch!

Flo raced back to Ramone's.

Ramone grinned when Flo pulled into his shop. "Is this my lucky day or what?" he said. But then he noticed Flo was upset. "How can I help you? I'll do whatever it takes to make you smile again."

"I've got a scratch!" cried Flo.

Ramone frowned. "Sorry, I can't help you," he said.

Flo gasped. "What's the matter? You're too good to paint me?" she asked.

"No, baby, you are too good for me to paint," replied Ramone, his headlights shining. "I can't touch a classic.

"Flo," he continued, "will you stick around Radiator Springs with me?"

Flo didn't need to think it over. "You bet, baby!" she shouted.

Moments later, Mitch and the Motorama girls showed up outside.

"Did you get that scratch fixed?" asked Rhonda worriedly. "Ms. Victoria is good as new. It's time to go, Flo."

Flo smiled at Ramone. "Sorry, girls, my touring days are over. I'm staying here in Radiator Springs."

"But why?" asked Laverne.

"Let's just say I've received a . . . more interesting proposal," Flo said with a wink.

And Flo and Ramone have been cruising together, low and slow, ever since.

And Now a Word from Our Sponsor

Once upon a time, there were two brothers named Dusty and Rusty. They owned a small company called Rust-eze. They loved nothing more than laughing, good-naturedly teasing each other, and telling silly jokes.

"When is a car not a car?" Dusty the van would ask.

"I don't know, Dusty," said Rusty. "When is a car not a car?"

"When it turns into a gas station!" Dusty would answer.

And the brothers would laugh and laugh.

Rust-eze was a popular medicated bumper ointment that claimed to get rid of embarrassing rust.

BEFORE

AFTER

One day, Rust-eze's longtime spokescar announced his retirement.
"What time is it?" Rusty asked Dusty, after the retirement party
was over.
"I don't know, Rusty," said Dusty. "What time is it?"
"Time to find a new spokescar!" answered Rusty.
The two cars laughed and laughed.

83

So the brothers held some auditions. Cars and trucks lined up and down the block to try out. But no one was quite right.

One car's bumper fell off in the middle of his audition.

Another kept forgetting her lines.

And one unfortunate car had an allergic reaction to the ointment!

"Knock-knock," said Dusty.
"Who's there?" replied Rusty.
"Orange," said Dusty.
"Orange, who?" asked Rusty.
"Orange you thinking that this audition was a complete disaster?" said Dusty.
The brothers laughed and laughed.

Rusty and Dusty sent out a memo to all the trucks that delivered Rust-eze across the country. It read HELP US FIND OUR NEW SPOKESCAR!

Mack was a truck who delivered Rust-eze up and down the eastern seaboard. There was nothing he liked better than to watch regional car races in his spare time. And his favorite race car of all . . .

. . . was Lightning McQueen. Boy could that kid race!

One day, Mack overheard McQueen's sponsor talking to him. McQueen was being dropped for a young hotshot named Smokin' Sammy Smelter.

"But his racing stinks!" Lightning said with a groan.

"Exactly!" the sponsor replied, laughing. "We're Smell Swell Deodorizer."

That's when Mack came rolling up.

"The guys I work for are looking for a race car to sponsor," he said. "Why don't you come back to Boston with me and you can meet with them, see if you like what they have to say."

McQueen blinked. "Are you serious?" he asked.

Mack nodded.

"All right! Boston here we come!" McQueen exclaimed.

The trip was a good one. McQueen and Mack swapped stories the whole way. They took a break at Mack's favorite truck stop, and Mack got to introduce his new friend to some of the big rigs he knew.

"Hi, I am a precision instrument of speed and aerodynamics," said McQueen.

"Well, I'm a precision instrument of pulling really heavy things," replied one of the big trucks.

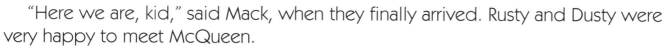

"Here we are, kid," said Mack, when they finally arrived. Rusty and Dusty were very happy to meet McQueen.

"The rain and snow are hard on us," began Rusty.

"This is very clear," added Dusty.

"But take some of our new ointment," said Rusty.

Dusty smiled. "And rub it on your—"

"So what do you guys think?" interrupted Mack.

"You're hired!" Rusty and Dusty cried, looking at McQueen.

"That's great!" said McQueen with a huge grin. "Um, what exactly will I be promoting?" He knew that whatever it was, it had to be better than car deodorizer!

"Oh, you'll be advertising Rust-eze Medicated Bumper Ointment's new rear-end formula!" exclaimed Rusty.

But after a quick glance at his new friend, McQueen knew what to do.

"As long as Mack can be my driver,
I'll take the job!" McQueen declared.

After McQueen nixed their first ad campaign . . .

Are your itchy RUST spots making you feel blue? Just slather on some **Rust-eze** And your rear end's good as NEW!

Rusty and Dusty came up with a new one that they all loved.

And best of all, Mack's new job was to be McQueen's driver!

Everyone was very happy.
"We have a new spokescar," said Dusty.
"And it all turned out fine," added Rusty.
"Just don't drive like my brother," said Dusty.
Rusty grinned. "No, don't drive like mine!"

Ciao, America!

"**A**rrivederci, Mamma!" Luigi called. He was about to set sail for the United States to work for his uncle, who owned a store called Casa Della Tires.

"Arrivederci, Luigi!" his mother cried.

Luigi was sad to be leaving Italy. But he was also very excited. He was on his way to the wonderful American city of Radiator Springs!

Luigi was standing on the deck, talking with another passenger about their favorite cars.

"To me, the car which is the best is a—" Luigi began.

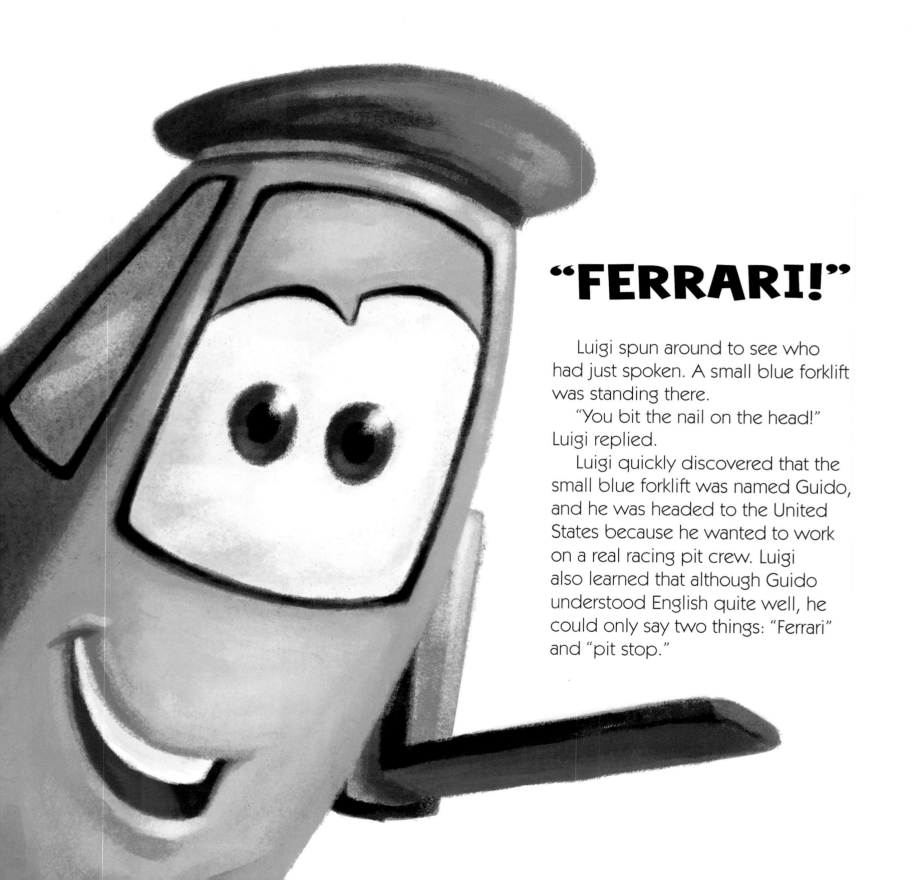

"FERRARI!"

Luigi spun around to see who had just spoken. A small blue forklift was standing there.

"You bit the nail on the head!" Luigi replied.

Luigi quickly discovered that the small blue forklift was named Guido, and he was headed to the United States because he wanted to work on a real racing pit crew. Luigi also learned that although Guido understood English quite well, he could only say two things: "Ferrari" and "pit stop."

Guido and Luigi became fast friends. Besides their shared love of Ferraris and auto racing, Guido was also great at making the long hours on the ship go by quickly.

And when the seas got rough, Guido and Luigi were the only two passengers who didn't get seasick!

After a long voyage, they finally arrived in New York City.

"Look, it is the Statue of Luberty!" Luigi shouted.

Guido and Luigi decided to go on a tour of the city.
They went to Central Park . . .

. . . the Chrysler Building . . .

. . . the Stock-Car Exchange . . .

. . . and Timing Belt Square.

That's where Guido helped a taxi change his flat tire.

"2.5 seconds flat!" said the taxi admiringly. "Must be some kind of record!"

Luigi was impressed. "You can fix very well the tires," he said. "I must to ask if you will come with me to the big American city of Radiator Springs."

Guido thought for a moment, then agreed.

"These are very good news!" cried Luigi. "My uncle, he will be very happy."

So they set off for Radiator Springs. They decided to take the scenic route. Luigi told Guido that they might even see a Ferrari on their travels! Guido was very excited at the prospect.

There was so much to see along the way! Their first stop was Niagara Falls. It was amazing. But there were no Ferraris to be seen.

Next they visited the St. Louis
Arch. You guessed it, no Ferraris.

Then they traveled to
Old Faithful.
"This geyser, I don't
know where is it," Luigi said.

Mount Rush Hour was magnificent, though both Luigi and Guido were disappointed that there were no Ferraris etched into the stone.

"The Golden Gate Bridge—*bellissimo!*" exclaimed Luigi.

120

Luigi wanted to see the Grand Canyon. It was very grand indeed. (Even though there were no Ferraris.)

Guido had one last request before they headed to their final destination. He wanted to see the glitz and glamour of Hollywood.

When the sun had completely come up, the two took off.

"We're almost there," Luigi said breathlessly. "I can't wait to see my uncle again. I am behind myself with excitement."

Finally they arrived in Radiator Springs.

"*Benvenuto!*" cried Luigi's uncle. He was very happy to see his nephew.

"*Ciao!*" said Luigi. "This is my friend Guido. He can change a tire in 2.5 seconds!"

"*Benvenuto!*" said Luigi's uncle, beaming. But Guido just stared at a bunch of tires by the store's entrance.

"You are liking it here, Guido?" asked Luigi worriedly. Was his friend homesick?

Guido still said nothing. But then *zip-zip-zip*, fast as lightning, he tossed a bunch of old tires into a leaning tower of tires. Then he smiled. A big smile.

Luigi's uncle was pleased. "We are a good team," he told his nephew. "We will be *molto* successful!"

Luigi smiled. "*Si*," he said. "Those tires, they are going to sell like fruitcakes!"

THE END